Lemon Sisters

Andrea Cheng

Illustrated by Tatjana Mai-Wyss

G. P. Putnam's Sons • New York

To the ten cousins: Jessica, Nicholas, Joshua, Matthew,
Jane, Rachael, Jonah, Ann, Rebekah, Jenny Kate—A. C.

To my parents—T. M.

G. P. PUTNAM'S SONS
A division of Penguin Young Readers Group
Published by The Penguin Group
Penguin Group (USA) Inc., 375 Hudson Street, New York, NY 10014, U.S.A.
Penguin Group (Canada), 90 Eglinton Avenue East, Suite 700, Toronto, Ontario, Canada M4P 2Y3 (a division of Pearson Penguin Canada Inc.).
Penguin Books Ltd, 80 Strand, London WC2R 0RL, England.
Penguin Ireland, 25 St. Stephen's Green, Dublin 2, Ireland (a division of Penguin Books Ltd.).
Penguin Group (Australia), 250 Camberwell Road, Camberwell, Victoria 3124, Australia (a division of Pearson Australia Group Pty Ltd).
Penguin Books India Pvt Ltd, 11 Community Centre, Panchsheel Park, New Delhi - 110 017, India.
Penguin Group (NZ), Cnr Airborne and Rosedale Roads, Albany, Auckland 1310, New Zealand (a division of Pearson New Zealand Ltd).
Penguin Books (South Africa) (Pty) Ltd, 24 Sturdee Avenue, Rosebank, Johannesburg 2196, South Africa.
Penguin Books Ltd, Registered Offices: 80 Strand, London WC2R 0RL, England.

Library of Congress Cataloging-in-Publication Data
Cheng, Andrea. The lemon sisters / Andrea Cheng ; illustrated by Tatjana Mai-Wyss.
p. cm. Summary: On her 80th birthday, a woman watches three young sisters play outside in the snow,
remembers good times with her own sisters, and receives several birthday surprises.
[1. Sisters—Fiction. 2. Birthdays—Fiction. 3. Old age—Fiction. 4. Neighbors—Fiction.
5. Snow—Fiction.] I. Mai-Wyss, Tatjana, 1972– ill. II. Title.
PZ7.C41943Lem 2006   [E]—dc22   2005002208

ISBN 0-399-24023-3
1 3 5 7 9 10 8 6 4 2
First Impression

My room is washed in light. I know, even without looking outside, that snow has fallen. My toes tingle like when I was a little girl, sharing the bed with my sisters, Rita and Mae.

Now I am alone, an old lady. I shuffle in my slippers to the window.
It is so bright, I can't see until my eyes adjust to the whiteness all around.

By the ginkgo tree I see three children wearing hats—one red, one blue, one yellow—and mittened hands already busy scooping, piling, dumping. They mound and carve and pat until they have a house around the tree trunk with one chair for each. Blue Hat is in charge, pointing this way and that.

I was like Blue Hat once, always the boss, telling Rita
what to do and she telling Mae, who followed along,
so happy to be part of our trio.

The three children sit down to rest. Blue Hat adjusts her armrest. Little Red
licks the snow. I open my window just a crack to hear their voices.

"Come on. There's work to do. We need a path to the store for later when
we get hungry."

"I'm hungry already."

"Then what are you waiting for?"

"Okay, let's buy some oatmeal."

With boots and sticks they carve a path from the ginkgo to the sycamore tree; then, back in their house, the chef stirs and stirs until the oatmeal thickens on the snow stove.

"Okay, it's ready, nice and hot."

"Yum. This is the best oatmeal I've ever had."

Rita and Mae and I once made real lemon ices in the snow. Mom cut lemons for us and Rita squeezed the juice onto the snow. I added sugar. Mae was the taster. A little too tart. Add some sugar, now more lemon, in layers, like a cake. Mae's mouth puckered like a fish.

The three workers are resting again. I go down into the kitchen and cut three lemons, one for each, and put some sugar in a plastic bag.

Then I open the door and ask,
"Would you like to make a lemon ice?"
They look at each other, remembering
what their parents have told them
about not taking things from strangers.
I want to tell them that I had
two sisters, that we were three
just like them. I offer again.

"It's okay," Blue Hat tells the other two. "I know her, sort of. She's lived here a real long time."

They don't even know how long, more than fifty years.

"How do you make lemon ice?" asks Little Red.

"Just squeeze the lemon onto the snow, then add some sugar, a layer of lemon, a layer of sugar, lemon, sugar, and snow on top."

They nod. "Thank you. Thank you. Thank you." Each mittened hand takes a lemon and I shut the door to keep out the cold wind.

I shiver and pull my robe tighter. I wish Rita and Mae were here with me to share a cup of tea. But Rita moved to Louisiana. Her handwriting is shaky now; she says she can hardly grip the pen anymore, so she just sends a card on my birthday. Mae, well, Mae went out all the way to California. They used to visit on my birthday, but they haven't come in years.

I watch the three children through the window, layering so carefully, sprinkling the dry snow on top. Now for the taste. Blue Hat goes first. "It's fantastic. Try some," she says. They take turns tasting.

My legs are tired. Even with
the tea I'm cold, so I go back up to
my bed and cover myself with all the
blankets. How did I get so old so fast,
I wonder. Can I really be eighty?
Rita is seventy-eight. And Mae,
the baby, is seventy-six.
I fall asleep remembering
my sisters breathing
beside me so long ago.

There is knocking on my door. I put my feet to the cold floor and make my way downstairs slowly.

The door is stuck with ice. It takes me a minute to get a good grip. When it finally opens, I see two old ladies wrapped in scarves.

"HAPPY BIRTHDAY!" they shout.
It can't be them. It's too cold to travel.
But when they hug me, I know that
Rita and Mae have come home.

"How long have you two been planning this?" I ask.

Their eyes shine. "Oh, a long time."

"And you never let on."

"Then it wouldn't have been a surprise, now, would it?"

Rita finds the cinnamon tea, Mae the plain. I already have my lemon. We sit around the small table, laughing and telling stories of long ago.

"So, how are we going to celebrate your birthday?" Mae asks.

"We *are* celebrating," I say.

Again there is a knock at the door.

"Now, who could that be?" I ask.

"We wanted to know if you could come out," says Blue Hat.

"We have a surprise for you," says Little Red.

I think for a minute. The wind is cold. The snow is deep.

We are three old ladies.

"Please," says Little Yellow.

Blue leads me, Red leads Rita, and Yellow leads Mae. "Close your eyes,"
Red says.

"But we might fall," I protest.

"Come on, now, what's a surprise with your eyes open?" says Mae,
so we do as we are told.

"Now sit," says Blue.
"Right here?"
"Right here."
I let my knees bend.

"Happy birthday!" shout the three children together.

I open my eyes. Each of us has a magnificent chair and on each armrest is a many-layered lemon ice.

"How did you know it was my birthday?" I ask.

They look at each other. "We have big ears," says Little Yellow.

"Just like we used to," I say.

"Isn't that the truth," says Rita.

I blow out eight stick candles. Each one stands
for ten, Blue says.

"How did you know how old I am?" I ask.

"Just guessed," she says.

"Do I really look that old?" I ask.

"Older," says Rita.

"Stop it," says Mae. "None of us are spring chickens."

"These are the best lemon ices I've ever had," Rita says.

"Me too," says Mae.

"This is the best birthday I've ever had," I say.

"Out of all eighty?" asks Blue.

I nod. "All eighty."